NAT the CAT'S Sunny Smile

Jez Alborough

To Sally

 *Nat the Cat's Picnic Song* can be heard
and downloaded, along with the sheet music,
from **jezalborough.com/natthecat**

NAT THE CAT'S SUNNY SMILE
A RED FOX BOOK
978 1 782 95129 2

First published in Great Britain by Doubleday, an imprint of Random House Children's Publishers UK
A Random House Group Company

Doubleday edition published 2013
This edition published 2013

1 3 5 7 9 10 8 6 4 2
Copyright © Jez Alborough, 2013
Nat the Cat's Picnic Song © Jez Alborough, 2013

With thanks to Philippa and Dave for help with the musical notation.

RANDOM HOUSE CHILDREN'S PUBLISHERS UK
61–63 Uxbridge Road, London W5 5SA

www.**randomhousechildrens**.co.uk
www.**randomhouse**.co.uk

Addresses for companies within The Random House Group Limited can be found at:
www.randomhouse.co.uk/offices.htm

THE RANDOM HOUSE GROUP Limited Reg. No. 954009

A CIP catalogue record for this book is available from the British Library.

Printed in China

FSC
www.fsc.org

MIX
Paper from
responsible sources
FSC® C104723

The Random House Group Limited supports the Forest Stewardship Council® (FSC®),
the leading international forest-certification organisation. Our books carrying the FSC label are printed on
FSC®-certified paper. FSC is the only forest-certification scheme supported by the leading environmental organisations,
including Greenpeace. Our paper procurement policy can be found at www.randomhouse.co.uk/environment

Nat the Cat jumped out of bed
with a smile spread halfway round her head.
She packed a picnic snack to share
with her friends Billy Goat and Hugo Hare.

With a smile on her face and hamper in paw
Nat **KNOCK KNOCK KNOCKED** on Hugo's door.

'**Hugo**,' she called, 'are you ready to go?'
but then, oh dear . . .

Hugo said, 'No!
My ears are all floppy,
I've lost my hop.
I want to get going
but my body says, "Stop".'

It's hard to feel bright on a day like today,
when the sky is so dingy, dreary and grey.
'I'm sorry,' he said, 'I don't want to be rude,
but Hugo is **not** in a picnicky mood.'

'Never mind Hugo,' said Nat the Cat
and she gave Hugo's head a **PAT, PAT, PAT.**

As Nat skipped away, Hugo felt strange,
the feelings inside him started to change.

His feet, which had stopped,
developed an itch.
His ears, which had flopped,
now started to twitch.
They began to point upwards,
they lost their flop,

then suddenly
Hugo went . . .

The grey in the sky
had decided to stay
but the grey inside Hugo
had all gone away.

A smile stretched out across his face
as he hopped and bopped all over the place.

Meanwhile, Nat was skipping along
swinging her arms and humming a song.

With a smile on her face and hamper in paw,
She **KNOCK, KNOCK, KNOCKED**
at Billy Goat's door.

'**Billy**,' called Nat, 'are you ready to go?'
but then, oh dear . . .

Billy said, 'No!
I'm having a horrible day today,
nothing seems to be going my way.
I stubbed my hoof
on the leg of a chair,
got soap in my eye
when I washed my hair.
You'd better just leave me here to brood,
Billy is *not* in a picnicky mood.'

'Never mind, Billy,' said Nat the Cat
and she gave Billy's head a **PAT, PAT, PAT.**

As Nat walked away, Billy felt funny –
as light as a feather and sweeter than honey.

And downwards from
his giddy head
this happy feeling
quickly spread –
until his tail
began to flap,

then suddenly
Billy went . . .

TAP
TAP
TAP!

He pranced and danced
all over the place,
as a smile stretched
wide across his face.

'This day isn't bad,' he cried. 'I was wrong.
It's been a wonderful day all along!'

On the path to the meadow Nat's feet felt sore
and the picnic seemed heavy to hold in her paw.

As she plodded along her wearisome way
she noticed the sky *was* gloomy and grey.

'What sort of a picnic,' thought Nat, 'will it be,
with nobody there to share it with me?'

Down in the meadow with blooms all around
Nat stopped by a lake and flopped on the ground.
The bumblebees buzzed, the dragonflies played
but Nat just laid by the snack that she'd made.

She felt like a car whose engine has stopped
or like a balloon that someone has popped.
Just then Nat heard a hoppity sound!
and the tap, tap, tap of hooves on the ground . . .

'It's us,' cried Hugo, 'but not like before,
I don't feel gloomy or grey anymore.'
'And I've lost my grump,' said Billy, 'Hooray!
After you left the grump went away,

and it's all because of your smile, you see . . .
you passed it on to Hugo and me.'

Nat the Cat sighed, her eyes opened wide,
they seemed to sparkle and twinkle inside.
She felt all dizzy, fizzy and yummy
as if someone were stroking and tickling her tummy.

Her frown turned around and there instead
a smile spread halfway round her head.

'Look, Billy,' said Hugo, 'we picked up the knack.
Nat gave us her smile now we've given it back.
I didn't know smiles could be caught like the flu.'
But he looked at Nat's face and he knew it was true.

Nat gave the snack that she'd made to share
to her friends Billy Goat and Hugo Hare.
And there round the blanket spread out by the lake,

they nibbled on biscuits and slices of cake.
And after they'd finished Nat made up a song
and both of her friends started singing along . . .

There's a pic - nic down in the mea-dow to day where the

bum-ble-bees buzz   and the dra-gon-flies play.   With

three hap-py friends,   Bil - ly,   Hu - go and Nat,   what a

won-der-ful pic - nic   it   is   to   be   at.

They laughed and they played and had lots of fun,
as the grey went away in the light of the sun,
which spread like the smile around the head
of Nat the Cat when she jumped out of bed.